Lighthouse Ghosts and Carolina Coastal Legends

The ocean's wild beauty evokes our most passionate feelings—the irresistible urge to see for ourselves what lies beyond the horizon, the insatiable human craving for new adventures, the noble self-sacrifice of putting our own life on the line to save others, and the hero's undying devotion to go far above and beyond the call of duty to protect and preserve our homeland. But it takes more than passionate feelings to overcome the arduous challenges of living and working on the oft-times inhospitable shores of the Atlantic. It takes a strong, indomitable will to survive.

In these pages you will meet some of the enduring spirits who have survived death itself and continue to live on in lighthouses, keepers' dwellings, and historic homes up and down the North and South Carolina coastline: long retired-but-not-gone keepers, a centuries-old Indian brave, a very lovely but very sad young woman, a little girl with a sharp eye for approaching storms, a young man determined to urge people to safety, a Civil War general, and a legendary seabird, to name just a few. Be sure to keep your eyes and ears open when you visit any of these places—you might just catch a glimpse, hear a whisper, or feel the presence of these enchanting, sometimes playful, sometimes compelling historical figures who will help bring the past to life for you.

CURRITUCK BEACH LIGHT STATION

A Nighttime Keeper and a Young Girl Linger at the Light Station

The Mystic Nature of Lighthouses Brings Back Keepers and Their Families

Before the members of Outer Banks Conservationists Inc. restored the keepers' dwelling at historic Currituck Beach Light Station, cold air filled the house during the winter months, pouring in through doorless entryways and paneless windows. Today only one room of the house still feels cold, and it feels cold all the time—not just when the outside temperature drops and not because doors or windows are missing or have inadvertently been left ajar. This room feels unnaturally cold year-round.

"People who tour the keepers' dwelling often remark that the upstairs bedroom on the north side of the house is colder than the other rooms," notes Lloyd Childers, who served as the executive director of the Outer Banks Conservationists and keeper of the lighthouse for many years. "Visitors sometimes tell me that they 'feel' something different in that room. Some visitors have refused to go in the room, and many that venture into the bedroom mention the coldness, not just as a temperature, but also as a feeling.

"I had just been here a short time when I decided to ask the board if they had anything to tell me about the bedrooms," adds Lloyd. "That's when I heard about the keeper's daughter story. The young girl went swimming in the ocean, and a wave caught her, and she drowned. Her body was probably placed on the bed for a time," she explains. "Perhaps related to that was an experience a guest reported in an adjacent bedroom. A woman was staying the night but couldn't sleep since someone kept pulling on the bedsheets. It was like a child trying to pull off the covers, kind of saying, 'Come play with me,'" Lloyd recalls. "We had not told our guest about the keeper's daughter's ghost," she notes.

"Perhaps the most startling experience for a guest was told by a man who also happened to be spending the night at the keepers' house some years ago. When he went downstairs to use the bathroom sometime after midnight, he happened to glance out the back window toward the tower and saw a keeper in uniform walking to the house. The keeper continued coming up the steps to the back door of the keepers' house and then just went right through the door—never opened it, never made a sound—just walked through the door as if it wasn't there," relates Lloyd.

This keeper, who has been seen before on the lighthouse tower stairs, may have come back to polish brass and keep the light in good working order. Currituck Beach would not be the first lighthouse where a dead-but-not-gone keeper lingers to assist in lighthouse duties. Similar stories have been told about New England and Great Lakes lighthouses.

Nearby Bodie Island Lighthouse, built from the same plans as the one at Currituck Beach, has *unscheduled* workers in the lantern room. Perhaps a keeper is filling in where he thinks he can help!

Keepers and their families began living in the duplex at Currituck Beach Light Station in 1876, the year after the 162-foot-tall red brick tower was completed. Employees of the US Lighthouse Service lit the lamps in the lantern room at the top of the tower for the first time on December 1, 1875, sending out a beam of light that filled in the last "dark spot" between Cape Henry, Virginia, and Bodie Island, North Carolina.

Over the past twenty-four years the Outer Banks Conservationists group has raised about $1.5 million from private donors to restore, maintain, and operate the lighthouse. It's no wonder that one—or perhaps more—of the keepers who devoted so much of their life's time and energy to maintaining and operating the lighthouse would want to stay!

The restored keepers' dwelling at Currituck Beach Light Station is home to the ghost of a former keeper. This view is from a window in the lighthouse that keepers enjoyed every day when climbing the tower.

The faithful keepers of Currituck Beach Lighthouse climbed these stairs every day. Dedication and perseverance evidently have induced strong feelings of "belonging" to the lighthouse because at least one keeper has decided to never leave his treasured post. These stairs are open to climbing—a highlight of visiting Outer Banks lighthouses.

Directions to Currituck Beach Lighthouse: Take Highway 12 north from 158 in Kitty Hawk to Corolla. The lighthouse is visible from the road on the left. Turn left into the light station's parking area. Phone (252) 453-4939 or visit http://www.currituckbeachlight.com.

KITTY HAWK
A Legendary Black Pelican Appears with Storms and Danger
Rare Seabird Has Reportedly Assisted in Countless Rescues off the Kitty Hawk Coast

When the hardy keepers and surfmen of US Life-Saving Station Number 6 put their own lives in danger to save ships' crews and passengers in peril off the coast near Kitty Hawk, they often got most welcome help from a most unexpected source—a rare black pelican.

W. D. Tate, the first keeper of the Kitty Hawk Life-Saving Station, "kept a journal of the bird's role as fearless 'watchdog' of the open seas," reports Lisa Haraburda, who has written an account of the Legend of the Black Pelican. According to Lisa's account, the unusually colored seabird first appeared during a nor'easter that wreaked havoc along the Outer Banks shortly after the life-saving station was completed and manned in 1874. As the storm bore down on the coast and visibility diminished, the pelican "with its magnificent wings parted and sleek body extended . . . swooped down" on the surfmen, alerting them that a vessel in trouble was fast approaching the shore. Thanks to the black pelican's deliberate, attention-getting action, Keeper Tate and his fearless men reached the storm's victims in time to snatch them from a watery grave.

The pelican continued to assist the surfmen not only by alerting them of impending disaster in stormy weather but also by actually leading them to shipwrecks "through blinding storms and turbulent waters." The black pelican was also often seen "gracefully coasting along the open sea air, its glance wary and posture alert" seemingly patrolling the coast for any sign of people in distress or threatening weather.

As Lisa records, over the years many people, especially grateful shipwreck survivors, reported that the "graceful, black-winged figure" had filled them with "a sense of hope and security," which encouraged them to hang on until the human lifesavers could reach them. For centuries the pelican has been recognized as a symbol of self-sacrifice and nurturing. During the Medieval Ages people believed that a mother pelican pierced her breast to feed her young, probably based on observations of an adult pelican pressing the pouch part of its long beak back against its neck to push the small fish it had caught out of the pouch and into the mouths of the young birds; the red tip of the pelican's beak and the reddish color of its breast feathers may have appeared to be blood to the observers.

The black pelican reportedly remained on duty at the 1874 US Life-Saving Station Number 6 until it closed in 1915. As Lisa notes, then the "sightings ceased, and the skies along the shore seemed so . . . empty. The pelican's duty as endearing scout" appeared to be over. Lisa adds that in the ensuing years the number of pelicans on the Outer Banks diminished greatly as environmental pollution and commercial development took their toll. Thanks to the efforts of conservationists and government-funded environmental cleanup and restabilization projects however, the brown pelican population in coastal North Carolina has "made a remarkable comeback—and symbolize a threatened species that now seems destined to survive," according to an article in the August 25, 1996, issue of *The Virginian Pilot*.

The Black Pelican Restaurant/Oceanfront Cafe and gift shop, in the restored and remodeled historic 1874 US Life-Saving Station Number 6, is near Mile Post 4½ on Beach Road (NC 12) in Kitty Hawk, North Carolina. For more information call (252) 261-3171 or visit the restaurant's Web site, http://www.blackpelican.com.

The black pelican has even been seen again! According to Lisa's account, boatmen in the Oregon Inlet area have reported seeing "a suspicious black bird" and fishermen have reported an "odd-colored pelican . . . suddenly appearing as a bold, striking creature flying nearby, ever-watchful of the boat's crew" when stormy weather approaches and the seas get rough.

Whenever you're in the Kitty Hawk area, be sure to keep your eye to the sky for a rare black pelican. Also be sure to stop in at Life-Saving Station Number 6, which has been restored and remodeled to house the Black Pelican Restaurant/Oceanfront Cafe, named in honor of one of the area's faithful, legendary lifesavers.

If you sit down and enjoy a memorable seafood meal in this historic building, you may encounter another one of Kitty Hawk's famous—or perhaps in this case, infamous—lifesavers: an assertive, self-assured young surfman who acts like he owns the place. He may be T. L. Daniels, a young surfman who according to some accounts died in a confrontation with Keeper James R. Hobbs in 1884. Nancy Roberts details the experiences a number of people have had over the years with this restless but harmless spirit in her book *Ghosts from the Coast—A Ghostly Tour of Coastal North Carolina, South Carolina, and Georgia*.

BODIE ISLAND LIGHTHOUSE
Is Some Long-Ago Keeper Still on Duty?

"Men" Have Been Heard in the Lantern Room Even When No One Is Supposed to Be There

The tall white and black-banded Bodie Island Lighthouse can easily be seen from Highway 12 at the northern entrance to Cape Hatteras National Seashore.

When Jerri O'Shell was leading visitors on a tour of Bodie Island Light Station in 1998, she and the people in her tour group heard—but did not see—at least one workman in the lantern room at the top of the lighthouse. Jerri wondered how the man, or men, had gotten up to the top of the tower since at the time the stairs were structurally unsafe and the lighthouse had been closed for repairs. In fact, a wire cage around the base of the staircase was padlocked to *prevent* anyone from climbing the stairs. Besides, there was really no need for workers to be in the lantern room since the light was automated and appeared to be in fine working order.

At the end of the tour Jerri told the National Park Service ranger on duty at the light station about hearing somebody—or somebodies—whistling and talking in the lantern room. He checked the work schedule and found no record of any workmen or other Park Service staff members scheduled to be in the tower that particular day.

Well maybe no one was *scheduled* to be there, but Jerri and others definitely heard human voices coming from the top of the tower and not just on that day—but on numerous other days when no one was scheduled to be there. Not only are these "workmen" not scheduled to be there, but no one ever sees them go into or come out of the entrance to the tower.

Perhaps these unscheduled helpers are faithful keepers from years gone by who have decided to stay on duty permanently. Given the long history of construction-related problems at Bodie Island Light Station, perhaps these dedicated men have taken it upon themselves to make sure the light stays lit no matter how unsafe the staircase to the lantern room is or whatever other problems arise at the light station.

The problems began long before the first shovelful of dirt was dug to begin construction on the lighthouse on Bodie Island (pronounced "Body" Island based on the original spelling of the name, perhaps for the family who may have owned the land). In 1837 the members of the US Congress approved the funds to build a lighthouse at the northern end of the Outer Banks, where "more vessels are lost . . . than on any other part of our coast"—but they ignored the strong recommendation of Lieutenant Napoleon Coste, who had inspected the area, to build it on Bodie Island and designated instead neighboring Pea Island, on the south side of Oregon Inlet. Debate over the exact site for the lighthouse, problems with acquiring the necessary land, and disagreements over the design of the tower delayed actual construction for about ten years.

The problems continued as workers laid the foundation for the original, squat, 54-foot-tall tower. The government overseer for the project, who didn't have any experience in building lighthouses, refused to let the contractor and his engineering team drive the piles needed to stabilize the structure in the muddy soil, ordering instead that it be built on an unsupported shallow brick foundation. Within a year one side of the tower had sunk about 12 inches. Despite costly attempts to straighten it, the structure continued to lean more and more precariously, forcing the lighthouse to be abandoned.

The second Bodie Island Lighthouse, an 83-foot tower completed in 1859, stood firm and erect on sturdy piles, but it didn't last very long either. In the fall of 1861 retreating Confederate forces didn't want Union troops to use the lighthouse as an observation post, so they filled the tower with explosives and blew it up. The dangerous stretch of coastline remained dark for more than ten years.

The view at right, looking up from the bottom of the spiral iron staircase in Bodie Island Lighthouse, appears to mimic the interior of a beautiful nautilus shell. Volunteers who keep the ground floor open for visitors have heard sounds of men working in the lantern room at the top of these winding stairs. In reality, no workmen were scheduled to work there, and no one came down the stairs or emerged from the lighthouse, which is locked at night. Legend has it that a long-ago keeper is still on duty keeping watch.

Directions to Bodie Island Lighthouse: From Kitty Hawk or Nags Head take NC 158 to NC 12 south to the Cape Hatteras National Seashore. About 10 miles south, watch for the tall lighthouse on the right; a sign marks the entrance to the light station. A visitor center and bookstore are housed in the double keepers' quarters.

Construction on the third Bodie Island Lighthouse began in 1871. This time the construction itself proceeded without any major hitches, but about a month after the lighthouse keepers first lit the powerful first-order Fresnel lens at the top of the distinctive 156-foot tower marked with horizontal black and white bands, geese crashed into the lantern room, breaking the window panes and damaging the lens.

With all the challenging obstacles they had overcome to light the light and keep it lit, it's perfectly reasonable to expect the lighthouse keepers who served at Bodie Island Light Station to want to continue to do all they could to make sure the light stayed lit for all eternity. And from the sounds of their whistling and chatter, they seem to be enjoying their life-after-death's work!

Diamond Shoals off Cape Hatteras
Ghost Ship Appears Off Cape Hatteras With All Sails Set But No Crew Aboard

The Carroll A. Deering *Is the Famous Ghost Schooner*

On April 4, 1919, in Bath, Maine, Annie Deering pronounced, "I christen thee *Carroll A. Deering*," as she scattered flowers over the bow of the five-masted schooner that had been named for her husband, Carroll. Less than two years later this graceful wooden lady earned the nickname "The Ghost Ship of Diamond Shoals" when she wrecked off the Outer Banks under very mysterious circumstances.

Surfman C. P. Brady sighted the vessel in distress "with all sails set" on the northwest point of the Southwest Diamond Shoals at 6:30 a.m. January 31, 1921. Brady alerted surfmen at the Cape Hatteras Coast Guard Station as well as fellow lifesavers at the Big Kinnakeet, Creeds Hill, and Hatteras Inlet Stations, and the would-be rescuers struggled to launch their power lifeboats in the raging high sea. After being washed back up on shore several times, the surfmen managed to power and row to the wreck. They found the schooner "driven high up on the shoal . . . in a boiling bed of breakers." Although they couldn't get close enough to read her name or board her, they painstakingly scanned the vessel for signs of life but found none. Boatswain John C. Gaskill reported that "she had been stripped of all lifeboats" and a ladder hanging over the side indicated that the crew had apparently escaped.

Two days later the Coast Guard cutter *Seminole* got close enough to report that "the surf was running high . . . and occasionally breaking over the schooner's poop. It was impossible to read her name, but it appeared to be a long one . . . ." On February 4 the cutter *Manning*, a wrecking tug, and several surfmen were finally able to reach the stranded vessel and do an onboard search. They reported that the *Carroll A. Deering* was "in fair condition although fast going to pieces. . . . All provisions, clothing, and supplies of the vessel have been removed" although some food had been prepared for a meal that was never eaten. Boatswain Gaskill noted in his report that "had the crew remained on board . . . they could have been rescued . . . ."

No members of the *Carroll A. Deering's* crew or any of her lifeboats were ever found!

For more than eighty years the untimely demise of the *Carroll A. Deering* has remained a mystery despite intense investigations by the captain's daughter, the federal government, and historians. The few facts that have been verified include: In September 1920 the ship set sail from Boston for Buenos Aires with a final destination of Norfolk. On the initial leg of her voyage her captain, William M Merritt, became ill and requested to be relieved of his duties. At Lewes, Delaware, Captain Willis B. Wormell replaced Captain Merritt, and Chief Officer Charles McLellan replaced S. E. Merritt, Captain Merritt's son, as first mate. As the voyage continued Captain Wormell privately confided to a friend and fellow captain that he did not trust his crew. As the schooner approached Cape Fear, she ran into a gale. When she passed the Lookout Shoals Lightship late in the afternoon of January 29, 1921, some members of her crew were standing on her deck, but there was no sign of Captain Wormell. That was the last time anyone was seen onboard the *Carroll A. Deering*.

Speculation about the fate of the crew and why they abandoned the schooner has ranged from mutiny and capture by Russian pirates (who had captured at least one other vessel in 1920) to the more probable although somewhat unexplainable abandonment of the disabled vessel and subsequent drowning of all the crew.

The Coast Guard dynamited the remaining wreckage of the short-lived, lovely *Carroll A. Deering* in the spring of 1921 to prevent her from endangering other ships attempting to safely navigate the Outer Banks. A part of her bow rested on the beach at Ocracoke for some time, and later hurricane-driven waters carried her up to Cape Hatteras, where her remains continued to prompt curiosity about the Ghost Ship of Diamond Shoals.

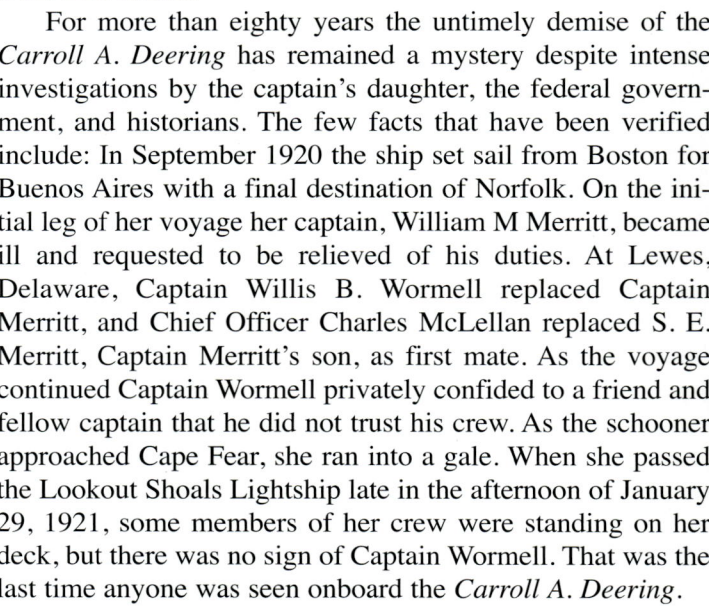

In her early days, the wooden-hulled, five-masted Carroll A. Deering *rode the waves at anchor near Bath, Maine, where she was built in 1919. On January 31, 1921, surfmen from the Big Kinnakeet, Cape Hatteras, Creeds Hill, and Hatteras Inlet Coast Guard Stations reported the ill-fated schooner stuck on southwest Diamond Shoals "with all sails set" but no one on board.* Photograph courtesy of the Outer Banks History Center

Cape Hatteras
A Lovely Lady Searches in Vain for Her Lost Portrait
Theodosia Burr Alston Has Been Wandering the Outer Banks Shores for Almost 200 Years

Poor Theodosia Burr Alston lost her portrait in a shipwreck in January 1813, and she has been looking for it ever since. Theodosia was sailing aboard the *Patriot* from Georgetown, South Carolina, to New York City to visit her father, Aaron Burr, when pirates attacked the small pilot boat just north of Cape Hatteras. Theodosia never made it to New York, and for the past almost 200 years she has been seen wandering the shore of the Outer Banks from Nags Head south to Bald Head Island, seemingly searching in vain for the portrait she was taking as a gift for her father.

No one knows for sure if Theodosia died in the pirate attack or if for some reason the pirates spared her life, allowing her to live out her days on the Outer Banks. One way or another though Theodosia's portrait made its way safely to shore, where it graced the wall of a simple cottage for many years. Eventually someone recognized the lovely lady as Theodosia Burr Alston and saw to it that the portrait reached its intended destination, New York City.

You can see Theodosia's portrait today at New York's Macbeth Art Gallery—and you may see the lady herself on the beach where Cape Hatteras Lighthouse once stood. Theodosia doesn't seem to know that her portrait has been removed from the Outer Banks for many people have reported coming upon this lovely forlorn lady, with her head down searching the shore as she walks along the shore from Nags Head southward to Bald Head Island. When you visit Cape Hatteras, watch for an ethereally beautiful young woman. She may appear to be even more forlorn than ever now that the lighthouse, with its comforting, welcoming, guiding beam of light, has been moved so far back from the shore.

You can read more about Theodosia Burr and Cape Hatteras Light Station in *Lighthouse Ghosts—13 Bona Fide Apparitions Standing Watch Over America's Shores* by Norma Elizabeth and Bruce Roberts. You can learn about how the lighthouse was moved in *Moving Hatteras: Relocating the Cape Hatteras Light Station to Safety* by Cheryl Shelton-Roberts and Bruce Roberts. For information about visiting Cape Hatteras Light Station, please call the National Park Service Visitor Center on Hatteras Island at (252) 995-4474.

Ocracoke Island
Ocracoke Preservation Society Conserves a House with a Ghost
Ghost with a Beard Brings This Home Back "To Life"

For the past twenty years the members of the Ocracoke Preservation Society have worked hard and accomplished much to preserve the historical, cultural, and environmental heritage of Ocracoke Island. This nonprofit, community-based group has rescued historic homes threatened to be destroyed by new development, raised funds to support the island's famous wild ponies, launched a number of photography exhibits, collaborated with the North Carolina Coastal Land Trust on the Springer's Point Preserve project, and developed a series of "Porch Talks" presented by authors, storytellers, musicians, quilters, National Park Service rangers, and local historians during the summer months to help island residents and visitors learn more about the area's rich past.

Perhaps the Society's diligent, highly successful efforts are preserving much more than just period photographs, documents, furniture, and other historical items. It appears that they are preserving not only *things* from the past but also a *man* from the past in their historic building.

The Ocracoke Preservation Society moved into the historic David Williams House in the early 1990s. Captain Williams served as the first captain of the US Coast Guard unit in Ocracoke Village when that service replaced the US Life-Saving Service in 1915. His family home, now in the town's historic district, was threatened by demolition to make way for new construction. The Society played a key role in raising the funds needed to move the century-old home to its present site on National Park Service property. The Preservation Society also raised the funds for and oversaw the restoration of the historic house and opened it to the public in 1992.

The first floor of the two-story home now houses a museum displaying historical exhibits that help bring Ocracoke's past to life. The second floor houses a research library as well as the Ocracoke Preservation Society's administrative offices. The second floor also houses an elderly man dressed in period clothing, and his presence truly does bring the past "to life."

Dee O'Neal, whose husband Earl's grandfather Isaac Willis O'Neal served at the Hatteras Inlet Life-Saving Station, describes the man from the past. "He is a very old man with a big, big bushy beard," reports Dee. "He wears a high-collared, old-fashioned coat and a stovepipe hat," she adds. "He appears in the upper right-hand window on cloudy, dismal, or rainy days. He always faces west across the 'ditch' (Pamlico Sound) toward the US Coast Guard Station. He holds a small, fluffy terrier in his left arm, which is crooked into a circle."

Mrs. Ellen Marie Fulcher Cloud, a native Ocracoker, was the first person to tell Dee about the old man in the upstairs window. Since then, whenever Dee is serving as one of the volunteer docents in the historic David Williams House, she tells visitors about the museum's living-history resident and suggests that when they go back outside they look up at the second-floor windows at the front of the house to see if he is there. A number of people have now reported seeing him, but no one knows for sure who he is or why he keeps looking out the window. Perhaps he is still waiting, hoping against all hope, for a loved one to come safely home from a fishing trip along the coast or a long ocean voyage. Or perhaps he is reminiscing about his own sailing days. Maybe he is the sole survivor of one of the many tragic shipwrecks that have claimed so many lives over the centuries off the treacherous Outer Banks waters.

The members of the Ocracoke Preservation Society warmly welcome everyone, no matter what their past, to visit their "home" at 49 Water Plant Road, near the National Park Service visitor center. They also heartily encourage anyone with photographs, documents, or anything else from Ocracoke's past to please contact them since, as their Web site notes, "we are always interested in expanding our historical collection!" And who knows? Perhaps the old gentleman who graces the upstairs window will turn up in one of those photographs and the society will finally have his name.

The historic David Williams House on Ocracoke Island has been preserved by the Ocracoke Preservation Society and is open to the public. The ghost of an old man with a big, bushy beard appears in the upper righthand window on dreary, weather-beaten days.

Ocracoke's Four Ghosts

On an island tucked away on North Carolina's Outer Banks is a village that has been compared to quaint Nantucket Island. Ocracoke has its own antiquity having been visited by early European explorers since Giovanni da Verrazano happened upon this long thin line of barrier islands in 1524. Legend has it that some who came to live here have never left because their ghosts revisit from time to time

What causes some spirits to return to their earthly homes and haunt their favorite places and what makes some people sensitive to their presence has long been the subject of intense paranormal studies. Whether you are a believer or a doubting Thomas, there are, nonetheless, countless stories with chilling reality about experiences of those who have seen these coastal apparitions.

Theodosia Burr Alston, beloved daughter of Aaron Burr, lost her life in a ship that sank off the Outer Banks. Visitors and residents have been recounting ageless stories about having seen her in a flowing dress with a sad face and they have even detected her distinctive, musky scent from Cape Hatteras to Bald Head Island.

An old gentleman with a big beard stands poised in the upper window of the Ocracoke Preservation Society's David Williams House.

Mrs. Godfrey returns to visit with guests at the island's oldest inn at the Island Inn and Dining Room, surely missing the guests she served years ago.

And the legendary, villainous pirate Blackbeard gives even the most skeptical a chill when they stand near Teach's Hole where he lost his head in his final fight to remain a pirate.

On your visit to the island, stand very still; let your senses try to detect the presence of any or all of these coastal legends.

Ocracoke Lighthouse is the oldest operating lighthouse in North Carolina. It is now part of the Cape Hatteras National Seashore and can be reached by toll-free state ferry from Hatteras Island. Although no ghosts have been reported inside the tower, several spirits, including Blackbeard's ghost, populate the island's ghost guestbook. The appeal of Ocracoke calls to all kinds of visitors, both modern day and distant past.

Directions to Ocracoke Island and Lighthouse: From the southern tip of Hatteras Island, take the state-operated, toll-free car/passenger ferry to Ocracoke Island (about a 45-minute crossing). After debarking at the ferry dock on the island, drive 12 miles south on NC 12 to Ocracoke Village. Turn left onto Lighthouse Road and continue until you reach a small parking area near the lighthouse.

Ocracoke Island

A Former Employee Refuses To Leave Ocracoke's Oldest Inn

Mrs. Godfrey Came Back To Stay and Entertain Guests

Dusk falls on the Ocracoke Lighthouse as seen across Silver Lake. Blackbeard's ghost has been reported in the vicinity.

Bob and Claudia ("Cee") Touhey know how a special place can take hold of your soul and keep on tugging until you come "home" for good. The couple had their first date on Ocracoke Island in 1978 and married in 1982. They chose to live on the mainland for a number of years—all the while dreaming of owning their own business and living at the beach. In 1990 they could no longer resist—they bought The Island Inn and moved their family to Ocracoke Island permanently.

Cee had lived on Ocracoke Island a few months a year when she was growing up. Her family owned a vacation home here, and she had spent many summers playing on the beach and, when she was a teenager, serving as a waitress in some of the local restaurants. During the 1980s Cee and Bob often brought their children, Mary and Russ, to Ocracoke Island for vacations. So moving here in 1990 felt a lot like coming home.

Like Cee and Bob, Mrs. Godfrey also came back "home" to Ocracoke Island and The Island Inn, and she appears to have taken up permanent residence on the third floor of the inn's main building. Unlike Cee and Bob however, Mrs. Godfrey's past experiences on Ocracoke Island were not very pleasant. During World War II she and her husband managed The Island Inn for owner Robert Stanley Wahab, and according to local history the couple "fought like cats and dogs." They went "down sound" to Cedar Island one night during the 1940s, but only Mr. Godfrey returned—or at least that's how it looked to most folks at the time. Actually Mrs. Godfrey did return home to The Island Inn—even though her body was left for dead on Cedar Island. No one was ever charged with her murder.

While Cee and Bob work very hard to make the inn's guests feel welcome and comfortable, Mrs. Godfrey seems to have taken it upon herself to entertain the inn's guests in unexpected ways. For instance she has been known to unroll toilet paper in the inn's private baths right before guests' eyes and slam doors to help ensure that their stay is unforgettable. And although Mrs. Godfrey is now an old woman, evidently she still enjoys "playing" with makeup, as one guest was "thrilled" to see in the middle of a most memorable night.

Cee and Bob look forward to warmly welcoming you to their home—your home away from home—on Ocracoke Island. If you spend the night in one of the rooms in the main part of the Inn, you may have the pleasure of enjoying some of Mrs. Godfrey's playful, attention-getting antics. If you prefer not to take advantage of the opportunity to enjoy that unique pleasure, you may choose to stay in one of the separate Island Inn villas across the street.

The Island Inn & Dining Room, which faces Silver Lake Harbor just down the street from Ocracoke Lighthouse in the community's historic district, is open year-round. For more information contact innkeepers Bob and Cee Touhey at (877) 456-3466 or visit their Web site, http://www.ocracokeislandinn.com.

OCRACOKE ISLAND

Blackbeard Can't Leave the Island Without His Head

His Ghost Has Searched for Centuries But Can't Find It

Restless men who live violent lives and die violent deaths are said to be some of the most restless spirits on American shores. Certainly among the spirits lingering near places of their deaths are pirates.

The pirate's motto was "A short but happy life," and this is exactly how Edward Teach, also known as Blackbeard, lived his turbulent life. He has become the most notorious pirate as the illusive master at hiding, perpetually moving to keep just ahead of authorities. He began as a privateer for England with permission to rob enemy ships. However, when his Letter of Marque was withdrawn, Blackbeard simply kept robbing and became an official outlaw-pirate. His choice of careers led him to an early grave off Ocracoke Island's shores, and today even the most doubting person feels a chill at the edge of Teach's Hole, the brigand's favorite lair at the southern end of the island where he met a violent death.

Why would anyone choose to become a pirate? During the early 1700s, it was not so much a choice as a necessity for many sailors. With no wars ongoing, countless sailors were out of work with no hope of income in Europe. Idle hands became mischievous ones, and piracy entered a golden age. Pirates frequented bawdy Caribbean taverns and lived aboard marauding ships. The object was to loot as many ships of their treasures and spend as much of the ill-gotten loot as possible before being caught and hanged.

Blackbeard's personality fits this character description to a "T," with his spendthrift reputation, intimidating tall stature, and heavy black beard and mop of hair that he sometimes set afire to scare his victims. His presence on Ocracoke Island has become legendary with countless tales about his ghost that continues to be felt. It is said he buried treasure including gold and silver at the southern end of the island on a spit of land that forms a lagoon called Springer's Point and still wanders the area looking for what must have been one of his greatest and dearest treasures—his head.

In a bloody, showdown fight on the morning of November 22, 1718, Blackbeard was mortally wounded near

Edward Teach, also known as Blackbeard, is one of the world's most famous pirates. Although Ocracoke Lighthouse was not built for a century after the pirate died, nearby is his favorite hiding spot at Teach's Hole—only a stone's throw from the lighthouse today. Photo courtesy of the North Carolina Division of Archives and History

Teach's Hole after seemingly superhuman strength carried him through stabs and cuts that would have brought a lesser man to his knees early in the fight. Lieutenant Robert Maynard of the Royal Navy was sent by a Virginian governor to capture the menacing pirate who had taken a toll on shipping. Facing the daunting task of overcoming one of the day's most infamous characters, Maynard finally overcame the feisty pirate, taking Blackbeard's head and its long, dark locks as reward. His head was hung on the bowsprit of Blackbeard's ship *Adventure*, and she sailed back to Virginia with it proudly on display. It seems the pirate is condemned to find his head—a remote chance at best.

It is advised that all heed the caution given in a rousing play by Julia Howard of the Ocracoke Preservation Society by one of Blackbeard's associates: "He'll never leave the island without his head. When the moon is full and shining like the devil's eye, don't go near Teach's Hole because the Captain will be there looking for his head."

Gold nuggets salvaged from Blackbeard's flagship, Queen Anne's Revenge, *are on display from time to time at the Maritime Museum in Beaufort, North Carolina.* Photo courtesy of the North Carolina Division of Archives and History

FORT MACON NEAR ATLANTIC BEACH

Civil War Long Past But One Confederate Still Makes "Appearances" at Fort Macon

Classic Coastal Fort Has Captured a "Feel of the Past." Palladium Windows and Stone and Brick Architecture Help Make This a Grand Home for a Confederate Ghost

Fort Macon still looks much like it did when it was completed in 1834. The outer walls of this pentagon-shaped brick-and-stone fortification are more than 4 feet thick, designed to withstand attacks from any enemy seeking to enter Beaufort Inlet, which leads to Beaufort Harbor, North Carolina's only deepwater seaport. Modifications made during 1841 and 1846 further increased the effectiveness of this crucial coastal defense.

The US Army Corps of Engineers built Fort Macon, and ironically US forces attacked and bombarded it during the Civil War. On April 14, 1861, just two days after Confederate sympathizers fired the opening shots of the war and forced the surrender of Fort Sumter, secessionist state militia forces based in Beaufort seized Fort Macon for North Carolina and the Confederacy. They successfully held this strategic position for a little more than a year, giving the Confederates a critical port of entry for much-needed wartime supplies.

By March 1862, however, Union forces had taken control of every major inlet through the Outer Banks except Beaufort, and Union Brigadier General John G. Parke set his sights on taking this prize military objective. After landing his troops on Bogue Banks and establishing a beachhead four miles from the fort, General Parke ordered his men to dig siege lines. On April 25, four supporting Union gunboats offshore in the Atlantic and floating batteries in Bogue Sound fired on the fort while General Parke's ground troops bombarded it with their large-bore, rifled artillery.

Using the heavy cannons they had brought to Fort Macon during the previous twelve months in preparation for the Union attack they knew would come sooner or later, Confederate Lieutenant Colonel Moses J. White and his men "easily repulsed" and "drove off" the Union Navy forces. But they could do nothing to prevent the extensive destruction caused by the more than 560 direct hits the fort took from the Union Army's rifled cannons. With seventeen of their defensive cannons disabled and the thick walls of the fort cracking around them, the Confederates raised a white flag and surrendered themselves and Fort Macon to General Parke on April 26, 1862. Union forces continued to control the fort for the remainder of the war.

You will learn more about the role Fort Macon has played as one of our nation's oldest coastal defenses as well as a civil and military prison when you visit the state park. Taking a guided tour of the fort, which is listed on the National Register of Historic Places, and viewing the historic exhibits and audiovisual displays will help bring the past to life for you here. And if a Civil War soldier named Ben makes one of his occasional appearances while you are walking the grounds or exploring the fort, you will have a most memorable living-history experience.

The park staff can tell you more about the still-lively spirit of Benjamin Combs, who died at the fort in the early days of the Civil War. Historical records indicate that Ben was hit in the back by a piece of shrapnel and "lingered" for at least several hours before his death. Evidently Ben has chosen to "linger" after his death too, and he seems to take delight in surprising the park staff as well as visitors from time to time. Although park staff members have never "seen" him, they suspect it was Ben who locked one ranger out of his office one day. Ben has also been known to slam doors and cut lights on or off, and reenactment groups who spend the night at the state park have reported "seeing something"—or maybe *someone*—around their equipment.

Ben always does subtle, playful stuff—never anything harmful or dangerous. And all a staff member has to say is, "All right, Ben, cut it out!" and the pranks stop—at least until Ben chooses to provide another living-history moment.

This palladium window is just one of the fine architectural details you will see at Fort Macon.

Fort Macon was the site of the Bogue Banks Range Lighthouses, completed in 1855 to mark the way into the harbors at Beaufort and Morehead City. Both lighthouses were taken down early in the Civil War to give Confederates a clear range of fire when defending the fort. In the picture at right, the curved stone entrance was designed to support the weight of heavy cannons. The cannons, like the one above, still give the fort a Civil War appearance, which may be one of the reasons our Confederate ghost makes it "home."

Fort Macon State Park is open year-round except Christmas Day. You can reach the state park, on the eastern point of Bogue Banks, by taking the bridge from Morehead City to Atlantic Beach and turning left at the light onto NC 58, which deadends at the fort. For more information about the state park, call (252) 726-3775, E-mail fort.macon@ncmail.net, or visit http://ils.unc.edu/parkproject/foma/history.html.

FORT FISHER AT KURE BEACH
The General Still Walks
The Last Rays of the Winter Sun Sometimes Reveal Images from the Past—Or Is the Vision a Wandering Reenactor?

This tall column marks the center of the original site of Fort Fisher. Federal Point Lighthouse stood nearby. The keeper's house became the fort's headquarters when Colonel William Lamb took command during the Civil War. He and his friend General William Henry Chase Whiting often met here.

Hope for the Confederate States of America died when General William Henry Chase Whiting and the Confederacy were mortally wounded in January 1865 at Fort Fisher, three months before the dogwoods bloomed in April at Appomattox. But as the revived historic fort lives on, so does the ghost of its famous Southern hero.

Several years after the Civil War ended, Confederate veterans of the last battle at Fort Fisher gathered at the ravaged fort to reminisce the horrendous battle in which they stood together and fought. Little did they know that they would be joined by an unexpected visitor.

It was near dusk when the figure of an officer climbed a gun emplacement near the old Wilmington road that wound its way to the fort's entrance. At first the group of veterans thought it was another compatriot who had come dressed in his old uniform to join them in their walk through the past. Just imagine their surprise when they saw general's stars on his uniform.

Mesmerized at the sight of the stately gentleman, they watched the hauntingly familiar man mount the parapet and look off in the distance as if trying to spot blockade-runners. Imagine how anxious this group was to speak with their hero, whom they affectionately called "Little Billy." They stood transfixed and paralyzed; then all at once the group burst toward him in welcome . . . but the general vanished. He was there one moment and gone the next. They looked in astonishment at one another, unable to speak. Then one veteran said in reverence, "That's the same spot where *he* was wounded." They knew it was General Whiting.

That sighting of General Whiting is not the only one. Others have seen him here—this is his place. He designed it and his good friend and military comrade, Colonel William Lamb, built it. President Lincoln's generals knew they would have to take it in order to end the war.

Fort Fisher had become the lifeline for the Confederacy once all the other Southern ports had been successfully blockaded. By 1865 more than half of the supplies needed by General Lee's Army of Northern Virginia, which protected the critical Confederate city of Richmond, were coming through the docks at Wilmington. Blockade-runners ran silently at night under the shield of Fort Fisher's guns at New Inlet entrance into the Cape Fear River on their way to port.

Whiting graduated from West Point with the highest grades ever made at the academy. His number one ranking in the class of 1845 earned him a coveted appointment to the Army's elite US Corps of Topographical Engineers. This group was America's first trained engineers, and they became the explorers of the West and builders of roads, harbors, and lighthouses of young America.

In 1859 Whiting left his signature mark on the Outer Banks of North Carolina by designing and supervising the construction of the 156-foot lighthouse at Cape Lookout, the first of the tall coastal lights in North Carolina and the model for Cape Hatteras and other tall towers built later. The original Cape Lookout Lighthouse plans, which bear Lieutenant William Whiting's signature, are preserved in the National Archives along with an index of letters he wrote during the tower's construction.

Although Whiting's stellar career took him to US Army posts around the nation, he married a young woman from a prominent Wilmington, North Carolina, family and over the years developed a deep love for the South. So when the Civil War broke out, he immediately resigned his commission in the US Army and accepted the position of major in the Confederate forces. Jefferson Davis gave Whiting a battlefield promotion at the Battle of Manassas from Major to General. Whiting took over command of the division in General Lee's Army of Northern Virginia.

When the final battle was approaching for Fort Fisher and there were no more reinforcements to send to Colonel Lamb, Whiting went himself and told his friend he was there to share the defenders' fate, all the while knowing they would be overwhelmed. Whiting was mortally wounded near the end of the fighting.

Today this land, which is wedged between the ocean and the Cape Fear River, is a state historic site just beyond the last beach houses at Kure Beach. In the winter it is quiet, almost lonely, down where the fort's headquarters once stood by the tall marker with an eagle on top.

Some say that if you wait long enough you will see a figure turn and walk toward the Cape Fear River and the setting sun. From a distance it is easy to tell the figure is an officer, and if you are close enough you will be able to see the general's stars on his collar. As lambent light from the setting sun flashes between the bare tree limbs, it seems at times to flow through the uniform. Then, at the crest of the low hill, the image vanishes! Only at that moment do you *know* it was no lingering Civil War reenactor in costume. It was General Whiting.

Whiting's spirit enriches this land, and his life was the stuff of legend. He has chosen to come back "home" to his beloved South and to his unfinished work at Fort Fisher. And he invites you to walk alongside him—or follow in his footsteps—as he surveys the fort's remaining defenses and scans the horizon for the first welcome glimpse of a long-overdue blockade-runner or the first unwelcome glimpse of a Union gunboat. Whiting is frequently seen at dusk and most often on cold winter days. Be careful to approach him slowly—and be sure to stay at a respectful distance lest he fade away to avoid capture and live to make his mark on living history another day. General William Henry Chase Whiting remains one of the South's most *enduring* historical figures.

Fort Fisher State Recreation Area, on the southern tip of Pleasure Island near Wilmington, is open year-round. In addition to preserving the remains of Fort Fisher, the area's pristine beach offers a relaxing opportunity to enjoy swimming, fishing, and observing sea turtles, shorebirds, and other wildlife. Fort Fisher also offers educational materials that correlate to North Carolina's competency-based curriculum in science, social studies, math, and English/language arts. For more information contact Fort Fisher State Recreation Area, P.O. Box 243, Kure Beach, NC 28449; (910) 458-5798; fort.fisher@ncmail.net.

Wooden palisades helped guard the land face of Fort Fisher; this section has been restored. The Cape Fear River flows in the distance.

BALD HEAD ISLAND

Theodosia, a Redhead, and a Man in a Pinstriped Suit Haunt North Carolina's Oldest Lighthouse

The Abiding "Presence" of Theodosia Burr Alston and Other Restless Spirits Add to the Irresistible Charm of this Island Oasis

The "denuded" dunes on the island's southern shore gave Bald Head its name. Its semitropical climate, breathtaking natural beauty, and more than 400 years of remarkable maritime history have given this island oasis its unique heritage. And its resident ghosts continue to give it extra-special charm.

Jane Carr Oakley, the former "curator of ghosts" for the Old Baldy [Lighthouse] Foundation and The Smith Island Museum of History, attests to the presence of at least three bona fide ghosts on Bald Island: the sad and lovely Theodosia Burr Alston; a woman with bright red hair who seems to be of Scottish descent and who may in fact be the very lively spirit of a Mrs. Cloden (sometimes spelled Cloadan or Kalodon); and a gentleman dapperly dressed in a pinstripe suit. Theodosia has been seen so many times by so many people over so many years that a bed-and-breakfast inn has been named in her honor, Theodosia's, where guests are invited to rock in the chairs and swing in the porch swings as they "relax and absorb the tranquil beauty of this seaside setting."

Poor Theodosia herself however seems to have a very hard time staying in any one place, let alone sitting still and relaxing. She is most often seen wandering alone and seemingly forlorn, sometimes along the beach, sometimes on the golf course near Theodosia's Bed and Breakfast, and at least once trying on someone's grandmother's wedding dress. People say that they smell a distinct musky scent before they see this beautiful young woman whose journey aboard the *Patriot* came to such an untimely and unpleasant end in January 1813. Theodosia was on her way from her home near Georgetown, South Carolina, to visit her father, Aaron Burr, in New York City, when pirates attacked the small pilot boat off the coast of North Carolina. The *Patriot*—with no living soul aboard—eventually drifted ashore near Cape Hatteras.

To this day no one knows for sure what happened to Theodosia. Did the pirates kill her along with the *Patriot's* crew and other passengers? Did she manage to escape from the attackers and make her way to shore? Or did one of the pirates take her to his Outer Banks cottage and allow her to live out her days in relative comfort but cut off from the rest of the world. All that is known for sure is that she has been seen myriad times from Cape Hatteras southward to Bald Head Island. She always seems to be searching for something—perhaps the portrait of herself that she was taking to her father in New York, the portrait that, apparently unknown to Theodosia, showed up years ago under somewhat mysterious circumstances on the Outer Banks and now hangs in a private museum in New York City.

Jane, who formerly gave historic tours of Bald Head Island (part of the Smith Island complex) since 1992, credits Cap'n Charles "Charlie" Norton Swan for most of what she knows about Theodosia. Cap'n Charlie served as head keeper of the Cape Fear Light Station on Bald Head Island from 1903 to 1933, and he told many stories about the lovely dark-haired young woman who wears a long flowing dress. While Jane hasn't personally "met" Theodosia, she and her husband, Doug, and their Siamese cat, Indigo, have indeed "met" red-haired Mrs. Cloden and/or the dapper gentleman in the pinstripe suit. These two "people" appear to have taken up permanent residence in one or more of the three restored/reconstructed keepers' dwellings at the historic light station.

Jane and her husband spent a weekend in the middle of the three dwellings. The minute they entered the two-story house, Indigo made a mad dash for the bed and crawled under the bedspread. The spooked cat, his eyes as big as saucers, refused to eat or drink anything the entire weekend, and he only came out of hiding at night. Jane and Doug watched helplessly as their scared pet gingerly crept from under the covers and "ran patterns" all the while howling mournfully. One night while they were trying to catch a few minutes of sleep in between Indigo's frenzied runs and pitiful moans, Doug "felt someone sit on the bed"—and it wasn't the cat.

Jane notes that another couple who spent the night in this very same house reported seeing the man in a pinstripe suit looking out the window toward Frying Pan Shoals. And when a family rented the house, their young son almost "drove his parents crazy talking about his invisible friend." He told them he met a "very nice" lady with bright red hair at the top of the stairs every night, and she would ask him questions. Jane also mentions the honeymooners who rented one of the other keepers' dwellings and were more than a little surprised to

Upon debarking the ferry at Bald Head Island, it only takes a glimpse of the old lighthouse to immediately feel the spirit of history that lingers here. The light was used to aid blockade-runners during the Civil War. Long before that though, Bald Head was home to several ghosts including the daughter of Aaron Burr, Thomas Jefferson's vice president.

Directions to Old Baldy Lighthouse and Bald Head Island: *The lighthouse can be reached only by passenger ferry from Southport, North Carolina. In Southport, turn west off NC 211 onto West 9th Street and follow the signs to the ferry dock on Indigo Plantation grounds. For ferry information call (910) 457-5003.*

see the bride's wedding gown "moving" while it hung in the bedroom closet.

When you plan your visit to historic, beautiful Bald Head Island, be sure to leave plenty of time to see Old Baldy, North Carolina's oldest standing lighthouse. Spend some extra time looking at the exhibits and talking with the staff at The Smith Island Museum of History, housed in one of the keepers' dwellings. While you're there you might just catch a glimpse of some of the island's most charming "residents."

For more about Bald Head Island (also known as Smith Island), contact The Old Baldy Foundation, P.O. Box 3007, Bald Head Island, NC 28461; (910) 457-7481; http://www.oldbaldy.org; keeperscottage@oldbaldy.org. For more about Theodosia's Bed and Breakfast contact the inn at Harbour Village, Bald Head Island, NC 28461; (800) 656-1812 or (910) 457-6563; http://www.theodosias.com.

PAWLEYS ISLAND
The Gray Man
His Appearance Is a Warning

Longtime residents will tell you for a fact that if you see the Gray Man and heed his urgent warning to leave Pawleys Island, you will be safe and your home will remain high and dry no matter how strong the wind blows, how hard the rain comes down, or how fast the floodwaters rise in the coming storm. What they can't tell you for sure is *who* the Gray Man is. Perhaps he is Perceval Pawley, the man who gave the island his name and made it his home. Or maybe he is Plowden Charles Jeannerette Weston, another resident who dearly loved his island home. Or, most likely, he is the man who died in a tragic accident on his way to visit his beloved in North Inlet in 1822.

Eager to reach her family's plantation as quickly as possible, the young gentleman was galloping through the marshland near Middleton Pond when he fell off his horse into quicksand. Sadly he sank in over his head before anyone could pull him out. A short time later when the heartbroken young lady saw a young man dressed in gray, she recognized him as her beloved, but he disappeared before she could speak to him. When the distraught girl told her family about the strange encounter, they decided to take her to the mainland to give her a change of scenery that would hopefully help restore her good spirits. Shortly after they left Pawleys Island, a hurricane struck that destroyed almost every living thing and almost every building.

Ever since then people have reported seeing the compelling young man dressed in gray and sensing he was warning them of approaching danger. Those who took his message to heart lived to tell about the tidal wave that swept over Pawleys Island in 1893, the tornado outbreak in April 1954, and the devastating hurricanes that struck in 1916, 1922, 1940, 1954, and 1989.

Just before Hurricane Hazel unleashed her fury on the island in the fall of 1954, the Gray Man came to alert a family who had rented a cottage for an off-season weekend getaway. The father reported being awakened sometime past midnight that Saturday night by someone pounding on the door. When he opened it he "saw a man who told him a storm was approaching and he needed to leave the island." Assuming it was someone from the Red Cross going door to door to tell people to evacuate, the father roused his wife and children, and they quickly packed their belongings into the car and headed toward the causeway—the only road off the island. When they reached the mainland, they saw a state trooper standing beside a barrier across the road. Surprised to see a car coming from the island, the officer asked them, "How did you know to leave? We didn't send anyone out to the island because no one usually goes there to vacation this late in the season—and since the roadblock was set up yesterday, no one has gone past me."

Just before Hurricane Hugo hit in 1989, a woman who had lived on the island for many years reported seeing the Gray Man for the first time in her life. Even though the weathermen had not yet told the public that a hurricane was approaching, she and her family evacuated immediately. Their house was one of the few left standing after the intense storm passed.

Local residents also tell about an elderly couple who were taking their daily walk on the beach in 1989 when they too saw the Gray Man. Knowing the legend and heeding the unexpected but timely warning, they packed their car and headed for the mainland. Hugo's storm surge ripped Pawleys Island in two—but when the couple returned home, they found their house just as they had left it.

When you visit Pawleys Island, take care to pay attention if the Gray Man comes to warn you—even if the sky is cloudless blue and the winds are calm.

Oak Island
Keeper's Ghost Returns to His Life-Saving Station
Keeper Dunbar Davis Wants His Closet Door Kept Open

When Judy and Gary Studer bought the 1882-style Oak Island Life-Saving Station in 1999, they wanted to preserve it—not transform it. An old keeper seems to like what they've done to his station so much that he's decided to move in permanently and make it a living-history house.

Judy describes how they first learned about their permanent houseguest. "The original keeper's room has a very heavy oak door," she explains. "We close it, but it opens 'by itself.' We are friends with Keeper Dunbar Davis's great-grandson, Joe B. Young, and when we told him about the door opening after we closed it, he said it sounded like his great-grandfather. 'He's definitely here!' he told us."

Keeper Dunbar was well known in Southport for his handlebar mustache during the years that he was head of the Oak Island Life-Saving Station. "It is his closet door that he insists on keeping open," Judy says. "Guests who stay in his bedroom find the door opening at all hours of the night no matter how many times they close it."

The Studers have beautifully restored the historic building to its former glory. Keeper Dunbar seems satisfied with all the restoration work and offers no objections to work done in other rooms of his Life-Saving Station. He simply wants his bedroom closet door kept open!

Judy and Gary Studer enjoy sharing the history of their house. If you are interested in learning more about this historic site, please contact them at jstuder@btdtgroup.com, garys@materialogic.com or (910) 278-9491.

Above is Dunbar Davis's bedroom in the restored Oak Island Life-Saving Station. His bedroom closet door is now kept open. Photo courtesy of Judy and Gary Studer. At right is a historic picture of Keeper Davis. Photo courtesy of Joe B. Young

GEORGETOWN LIGHT STATION

"Go Home!" Warns Little Annie

The Ghost of a Young Girl Appears to Sailors Whenever a Bad Storm Is A-Brewin' off the South Carolina Coast

One of America's oldest legendary lighthouses stands tall at Georgetown, South Carolina. This remarkable survivor of countless and ruthless hurricanes and severe floods since 1812 had an earlier companion that fell victim to a harsh gale in 1806. The first lighthouse disappeared, but after its demise, an ancient mariner's angel of mercy appeared to warn mariners of future threats. Annie comes to sailors who are within her protection. If they are wise, they will heed her stern warning and "go home!"

The Georgetown Lighthouse as it appears today.

Captain Sandy Vermont still vividly recalls the day in October 1954 when little Annie told him to "go home!" Sandy, who was a teenager at the time, was serving as the cook on Captain Mead's shrimp boat, the *Captain Dawn*.

"Everyone looked up to Old Captain Mead," notes Sandy in his thoughtful, soft-spoken way. "His boat was always the safest, he worked the hardest of any captain, he was a taskmaster—so his crew worked the hardest too, and he was wise beyond his years."

Sandy remembers the good advice his father gave him before he joined Captain Mead's crew. "He always told me to do something better than anyone else could, and I could put out a biscuit better than most," Sandy explains. He notes with pride that Captain Mead and his hardworking crew relished the hot biscuits he baked to go with their usual fare of sausage, beans and rice, fresh-caught shrimp, and strong coffee.

Sandy recalls that Captain Mead and his crew had fished the waters off the South Carolina coast south of Charleston that fateful fall day. That evening, after the hungry sailors had devoured every last morsel of the savory meal Sandy had cooked up on the galley's gas stove, he carried the cooking pot, which had "sooted up real bad," up to the stern starboard deck to clean it. While he was rubbing sand over the pot and rinsing the soot off with water, a little girl with long blond hair and gray misty-blue eye appeared before him. "Sandy, go home!" she warned.

Startled but not afraid, Sandy asked, "Missy, what did you say?"

"Sandy, go home!" the little girl repeated emphatically before she disappeared into the salty night air.

Not quite sure what to think, Sandy went to the pilothouse and told Captain Mead about his curious encounter with the little blond-haired, blue-eyed girl. Sandy barely finished his story before the wizened old sea captain declared, "You saw Annie. A storm's a-brewin'. We're going home!"

Without wasting another minute Captain Mead turned the wheel and set a course for Georgetown, their homeport. He ordered Sandy to tell the rest of the crew to pull in the nets and ready the boat for the 40-mile run to safety. While Captain Mead's steady hands guided the boat gently but firmly through the rising swells, Sandy used a bullhorn to call out to the crews of passing shrimp boats—one from Charleston and four from Georgetown. "I saw Annie," he warned them over the waves. "A storm's a-brewin'. Go home!" Only one captain scoffed at the message and kept heading out to sea. All the others turned back.

Thanks to little Annie's warning, Captain Mead and his crew, Captain Teddy and the crew of the *Morningstar*, and the others who heeded the little girl's words had enough time to not only reach Georgetown but also sail on up the Black River to safe storm anchorage. "With the storm fast on our heels, we scrambled to secure the boat's four anchors before we jumped into our small skiff and rowed to shore," recalls Sandy. "Our boat held fast in Hurricane Hazel. All the ships but one—the one whose captain refused to heed Annie's warning—rode out the storm in safety.

Sandy wanted to know more about Annie, the little girl who had literally saved his life and the lives of countless others. He asked Captain Mead, but the old seaman wouldn't talk about it—not until years later.

"One night I was sitting on the deck of my own shrimp boat tied up to the trees at Big Pine Dock in Beaufort when Captain Mead came by to help me mend nets, something he did from time to time," Sandy explains. As the two were working, Captain Mead, who was not a man of many words, cut his eyes at Sandy and asked, "Yah still want to know?" That look, seared for all time in Sandy's memory, left no doubt what Captain Mead was referring to. Sandy nodded yes, and the old captain started telling the story.

"In 1801 there was a wooden lighthouse tower on North Island," Captain Mead told Sandy. "An old keeper with the last name of Kruger lived on the island with his granddaughter, whose name was Annie. Her parents had been lost at sea. She was the only family he had—and he was the only family she had. From his watchpost at the top of the tower, her grandfather kept a close eye on Annie as she played on the beach and swam with the dolphins. Together they tended the garden and house and caught crabs for dinner. And Annie helped him round off the corners on the lamp wicks, polish the mirrors and glass, and clean the soot off the windows in the lantern room.

"Once a month Annie and her grandfather rowed their dinghy across the 11 miles of open water up Winyah Bay from North Island to Georgetown to shop for supplies. They would go in with the tide and out with the tide," continued Captain Mead. "Annie especially liked reaching her hand into the candy barrel at the general store and pulling out a treat. One day Annie went outside the store to wait while her grandfather finished shopping. She loved playing with the other children and the puppy dogs—something she didn't have on the island.

"Almost immediately though she came running back into the store and started tugging on her grandfather's sleeve. 'Papa, Papa,' she cried, 'the birds are flying high, and the western sky is red. We got to get back to light the light. There are men in the ocean—they will need it before night!'

"The old man didn't even stop to pay the bill or gather their things. He told the shopkeeper they'd be back later—they had to go light the light. He and little Annie ran back to their dinghy. The rain had already started, and Annie's grandfather pulled on the oars as hard as he could in his struggle to make headway against the incoming waves, which were

Captain Sandy Vermont, a seasoned sailor as well as a natural historian, talks about how Annie saved his life and shares other seafaring stories with passengers he carries on tours of the Georgetown and Cape Romain Lighthouses. To find out more about the tours, contact Captain Sandy Vermont at P.O. Box 186, Georgetown, SC 29442; (843) 527-4106.

already beginning to swell. Annie cupped her little hands and kept bailing the water that was fast filling their little boat, urging her grandfather to row harder and harder. 'We've got to light the light,' she kept telling him.

"Before they could reach their island home a huge wave crashed over their little boat and washed Annie overboard. Her distraught grandfather jumped into the churning waters and managed to grab the little girl before she was swept away. Holding Annie tightly in his big, strong right arm, he swam as hard as he could for the island—but little Annie pulled away. 'I'll go now—and I'll tell at least one man on one boat when a storm is coming. You'll never have to light the light again, Papa!' she called to him as the waves swept her out of reach that dark, stormy night on Winyah Bay."

Captain Mead paused before continuing, "My grandfather was the first one to check on Keeper Kruger and Annie after the storm passed. As he rowed toward North Island he saw that the lighthouse tower had been blown over by the wind, and when he reached shore he found the old keeper lying face down in the sand. He was still alive, but there was no sign of Annie. The heartbroken old man never left the island again. Ever since that tragic day, whenever people see the little dinghy head toward shore they know it portends a coming storm. And just as little Annie promised her Papa, he never had to light the light again in the Georgetown tower to help guide sailors to safety. She tells at least one man on one boat to 'go home!' whenever a storm's a-brewin'."

Hilton Head Island
Hilton Head Is Hauntingly Rich in Beauty, Heritage, and Spirits
A Young Woman in Blue and a Yemassee Brave Who Linger about the Harbour Town Lighthouse Attest to the Island's Long-Lasting Appeal

At right is the beautiful Harbour Town Lighthouse on charming Hilton Head Island, South Carolina. It is said that several ghosts haunt the site including a mournful Yemassee Indian brave who returned from a hunting trip to find his tribal home and family destroyed. Below is the original Hilton Head Lighthouse, which stands on a golf course nearby. Keeper Adam Fripp went beyond his physical capacities to carry out his duties during a hurricane and died in the lantern room. His devoted daughter, Caroline, remained on duty for several days and kept the light lit during the dangerous storm that threatened to topple the tower. Visitors have reported seeing her in a flowing blue dress, evidently still carrying on in her father's dedicated footsteps.

Once you step foot on Hilton Head, this beautiful island will become part an integral part of you. And if you leave for some reason, unforgettable images of its rich natural beauty and stories from its rich cultural heritage will haunt you, drawing you back again and again—until perhaps, like the young woman who wears a blue dress and the proud Yemassee brave returning from a very successful hunting trip, you will come back and stay forever.

Nadia Wagner, the current "keeper" of Harbour Town Lighthouse and one of the area's tour guides, enjoys sharing the stories of people who lived on this beautiful island in days, even centuries, past. Nadia notes that although the 90-foot-tall red-and-white Harbour Town Lighthouse was built a little more than thirty years ago as part of the modern Sea Pines Plantation community, it stands on ancient Native American tribal land. The Yemassee and other tribes settled on Hilton Head thousands of years before English sea captain William Hilton surveyed this 12-mile-long barrier island and gave it his name in 1633.

Nadia tells the story of one Yemassee brave who apparently has chosen to continue to live here even though the rest of his tribe departed many, many years ago. The young man left his family in the safety of the tribal village on Calibogue Sound one August night when he and other braves went to hunt game and catch fish. Five days later as the men slowly approached the island in their heavily laden canoes, filled with enough fresh meat and fish to feed everyone in the village, they were alarmed to see no campfires burning and no one waiting for them on shore. When they beached their canoes and saw the seaweed and broken tree branches littering the sand, they knew what had happened—a sudden, powerful storm had blown in off the big water and destroyed everything in its path. Overcome with grief the Yemassee brave laid down on the very spot where he had bid his family good-bye five nights before—perhaps the very spot where Harbour Town Lighthouse now stands at the entrance to the Sea Pines Plantation harbor—and willed himself to die.

Nadia along with many others have felt the presence of this distraught Yemassee brave and heard his low, sad moans. He seems to wander near Harbour Town Lighthouse, occasionally venturing inside, in his never-ending search for